MEMOIRS

OF

HOME

First published in the United Kingdom in 2022
by Daniel J Knight Publishing and Amazon KDP

Copyright © Daniel J Knight 2022

Cover images courtesy of:
Shutterstock

The right of Daniel J Knight to be identified as the author of the work has been asserted by him in accordance with the Copyright, Designs and Patents Act 1988

All rights reserved. No part of this publication may be reproduced, stored in a retrieval system, or transmitted, in any form or by any means without the prior written permission of the publisher, nor be otherwise circulated in any form of binding or cover other than that in which it is published and without a similar condition being imposed on the subsequent purchaser.

All characters in this publication are fictitious and any resemblance to real persons, living or dead is purely coincidental.

Paperback ISBN – 9798802637173
eBook ASIN - B09XY4LN4R

Daniel J Knight Publishing
United Kingdom

BY
DANIEL J KNIGHT

For Kirsten and for Cory,

    When all else fails, you are my guiding light.

    My purpose and my fire.

    Forever.

"Disasters work like alarm clocks to the world; hence God allows them. They are shouting, 'Wake up! Love! Pray!'"

- Criss Jami, Killosophy

INTRODUCTION

It never sunk in, that the gap between my last and first step on this planet, was 150 years, give or take. I was asleep for what seemed like an instant… a mere blink of an eye. A nap, even. But then, there I was, back where everything ended. Back where we said goodbye, and back to a place I barely even recognised.

The world around me had grown, and not in a way I'd ever hoped for. Moss climbed what structures still had the strength to remain vertical, and the sky seemed to dwell in a miserable blanket of grey.

Only small, fragmented intersections of the blue sky behind the clouds would poke down upon me as if as a whole, it were wary of its visitor. I couldn't tell you the number of times in the journey home I'd sat and stared from the windows. The pictures I painted in my head were… well… they were less shy of colour than our once blue and green rock, to say the least.

I guess there's no sense in me starting with riddles. There was just that… impulse to put literal pen to paper, you know? Record it all. Everything that's happened, if you were born into it, you'd never know how different it all once was before. In a way, that's what this is for: an insight into what civilisation was like before it all. A memento of times removed… if you will, so you can see what life was like before. A life I once lived.

You can call me Ned. Ned Sawyer.

My friends used to call me Noddy, so I guess you have can have your pick of whatever you want to call me. Hmph, I'm probably not even around by the time you read this anyway. Perks of this new era we live in. Nothing's ever certain, not even life. That's something we all found out the hard way.

And that leads me to the main attraction.

Earth.

Or what was left of it.

I've been off the ship no longer than thirty minutes. Half an hour, that's all, but the first thing I did when I got off, was run. I meant no disrespect by it, but I couldn't be around those people anymore. They were strangers to me, almost, in comparison to what I'd been removed from… and I had a home to go back to, an old life to rebuild. The house I grew up in was within my crosshairs, and I wanted everything it once gave me, back. Not just to rekindle with memories I held tight, but to live it all again.

At least, I thought it was that simple.

I'll take you back to where it all started, with the Titans, and I'll try my hardest to keep everything in an appropriate order, even if it is a bit difficult to do when everything I turn and look at seeks to trap me in a state of remembrance. Not even the good kind, mostly.
A bundle of call-backs wrapped up in a neat little ribbon, deceptive - as it would tear down my guard, every... single... time.

So, gear up, friends.

It's about to get rough.

"Without memory, there is no culture. Without memory, there would be no civilization, no society, no future."

- Elie Wiesel

ENTRY 1
ABSOLUTE

E arth's atmosphere was different to the ship's. I'd not taken a breath on this planet in over 150 years. But as I sat, perched on a rotted stone bench, and opened this journal, the memories of a life I once took for granted came flooding back, with a force so brutal it spun me about.

As you'd remember, thirty minutes prior, a bit longer at this point, I took my first steps out of Titan1, our barge.

A ship so massive it housed 15,000 of us for over a century. One of ten different barges that saved the few who were left when the world threw a tantrum because we didn't just ignore the signs that we were destroying our planet, we went as far as to test the legitimacy of every single claim that was thrust upon us.

You know how we humans are; we would never for a second believe something until we saw it ourselves, with our own eyes. But as early as 1896, Svante Arrhenius warned us of the effects our careless actions could bring. That was a century before we left, and in that time, we'd proved him… and everyone else that followed his in his footsteps, right about it all.

Ice caps began to melt. Water levels began to rise so high that continents appeared to shrink beneath them. Freak earthquakes, superstorms, and tsunamis wiped out chunks of the population at a time.

Slowly, but surely, we broke the very thing we took for granted: our home. It wasn't impossible to survive, not at first, but as was the case with everything that involved humans… it escalated pretty quick. We'd caught wind of the numerous claims, and seen countless news reports along the way, each with the same announcement of impendence.

'A superstorm of gargantuan and destructive proportions,' they called it. That's what was brewing in the wake of nature's disturbance. A whirling storm that grew above the horizon, of incomprehensible nature and mass. Of course, humanity shifted their levels of fear up a few notches. If anything could hold the power of feeding fear to the masses in such an effective way, leave it to the news.

When the reports wouldn't cave and panic across the planet united, our governments did, too. They poured trillions of their own currencies all into one single pot they'd use to fund what they would call the 'Titan Initiative."

Ten city-sized behemoths that would make you question physics just by looking at them. Each with the space to house 15,000 total civilians. Obviously, didn't include the crew, but even still, it hardly narrowed the numbers down.

At first, the Titan Initiative was deemed lacklustre by the public, naturally, given Earth had billions of people on it. But, soon enough, with every fit mother nature threw, and every monsoon of chaos that followed, those numbers dwindled heavily… until only shy of a million people were left standing, vulnerable to the world's drama. Those statistics alone put the fear of God in every man, woman and child that remained. And they were all susceptible to a near apocalyptic-level storm that was less than a couple of years from reaching its precipice.

Still, almost a million lives weren't about to fit onto ships that could hold not even a fifth of that in total. There also was no time or resources to build any more Titans, because of the massive cost to make them. That's when the shadiest suits started to bring down the metaphorical hammer. Selfish and egotistical enough to call themselves 'saviours,' their actions demanded an opposing label from the public.

Before they sent out their Titan admission tickets, which we all had to sign if we were lucky enough to be in receipt of - or else we couldn't board when the time came, they decided to narrow down the numbers in a messed up, discriminatory, and wretched way.

If you had a terminal illness, you couldn't board even if you wanted to. If you were over the age of 50, you couldn't grab a seat on the ride to survival, and if you had a disability of any kind, mental or physical, well… apparently that put the future of humanity at a huge disadvantage when it came to potential reproduction. So, you were robbed of even the chance of a ticket.

It was a relentless call that served to shun so many people we loved and cared about. And when the forms came through the letterboxes and we had to open them in front of our grandparents, and disabled or ill loved ones, it tore us all to pieces.

We had no say in the matter, either. Any arguments were pushed to the side. Petitions were thrown in the bin and protests were punished with threats of ticket expulsion. Safe to say, some of those invited onto the Titans tore up their tickets and chose to stay with those they loved. To see out what was quite possibly the end of their days, with the people they held closest, and personally, I not only understood them but felt the exact same way about it.

Me though, I had almost nobody left. I'd already lost my parents to the chaos that had been brewing prior to the announcements, and my grandparents... they wouldn't see me throw away an opportunity to survive, not even as I begged them to let me stay with them.

They sat me down at the kitchen table and personally handed me a pen as I simpered over the forms. They'd lost enough by then; they didn't want to see their time out with the knowledge that my future ended with theirs when it could be preserved.

So, I signed. As much as my hand pulled away from that piece of paper that hundreds of thousands of people coveted, my heart pushed it right back as I saw the looks on the faces that watched me.

And that was that.

Signed, sealed, delivered by my grandad on his way to work that afternoon. It didn't matter how bad I wanted to stay... their want for me to escape what was coming, and survive, heavily outweighed whatever I was feeling.

I loved them, dearly. As anyone would their grandparents. But even after all the reasoning and pleas, I still felt the waves of guilt ride over me in the knowledge that I had signed my name.

Then,

    Titan1 would call to me sooner than I thought.

"One can see from space how the human race has changed the earth. Nearly all of the available land has been cleared of forest and is now used for agriculture or urban development. The polar ice caps are shrinking, and the desert areas are increasing. At night, the earth is no longer dark, but large areas are lit up. All of this is evidence that human exploitation of the planet is reaching a critical limit. But human demands and expectations are ever-increasing. We cannot continue to pollute the atmosphere, poison the ocean, and exhaust the land. There isn't any more available."

- Stephen Hawking, Physicist and Author

ENTRY 2
TITAN

One year, seven months, and twelve days. That was how much time passed between the moment I'd signed the papers, and the day I was called to board Titan1. It was much earlier than expected, but so was the arrival of the superstorm, and it was destroying everything in its wake.

Cities, towns, everything. It was in moments like that; when you saw the footage on the news, that you realised exactly what they meant by the devastation it would brew. Without a Titan taking you to safety off-planet, there was no way you'd survive something like that. The storm itself was the size of an entire country. Quadruple the size of the ones that had already scarred us, and it was merging with the others. Soon, the storm would engulf the planet. The world wasn't about to 'end,' but the people sure were.

Even when temporary, the mood swings that mother nature can throw are some of which the devil would only dream of.

I'd never hugged my grandparents so tight, and for so long. My heart… well I'd never felt it so heavy; it dragged the entire weight of my body into the clutch of their shoulders and kept me there like I was pulled into it by an anchor. I didn't know how to handle the insane amount of emotion that invaded every ounce of my being.

"It's alright, sweetheart," said my nan. "We'll be right here when you get back."

I knew they wouldn't be. That her words were chosen to comfort me. I knew what boarding day meant, but still, I let her words ease me as I kissed both her and my grandad on the cheek.

It was the first time in a while I'd seen my grandad smile. He never spoke much, but that's why his smile was enough.

Then he said, "It won't be forever."

"You two behave yourselves while I'm gone, alright?" I joked as I walked the down path of the garden, to the bus that sat outside, right by the kerb in wait for me.

The path of the garden, as short as it was, had never felt so long before. It was like it didn't want me to leave. Like, rather than concrete slabs, it was a treadmill or some kind of conveyor belt that kept me in one position no matter how many steps I took. But in time, I made it through the gate.

Jupiter Avenue had never been so… empty. England's count of live bodies had dwindled so low that it took just one and a half Titans to contain all of those that remained there. And we were the lucky ones; some entire *cities* out there had been completely wiped out until nothing remained.

I found my seat on the bus. Stained, as was the lumpy lino floor I walked. It was an old bus, like something that would have taken me to school in my younger, infant years. The stench of oil and body odour took over me like an evil spirit. Clearly, their funds were spent elsewhere.

Nevertheless, as I perched on the seat beside a woman I'd never met before, in a bus full of people I'd only ever caught a glance at in the streets, I stole a look through the window left of me and watched as my grandad hung his arm around my nan's shoulder. My eyes were glued; I couldn't remove them, then again, I didn't want to. I knew it would be the last time I'd see them, to look away would be to rob myself of the people I loved. Either the driver ripped my stare away at the slam of his accelerator, or he'd find me climbing from the window to join them, as I wanted to.

One final wave, that's all I was able to give them as the bus left my home and my street. Every stop between there and the boarding location, I only prayed that someone I knew walked through its doors.

I knew it wasn't the only bus; there were a few of them running routes. But so far, I'd been stuck in a rolling metal container with people I didn't know, or at least, never spoken to, and didn't want to, either. I already had to make peace with the fact the best person I knew, my best friend, Emily, was about to board Titan4 miles away outside the town. At least, with her, it all wouldn't have seemed so bad. When the Titan

Initiative was announced, me and her crossed our fingers and hoped that if it ever came to be, we'd both be on the same Titan, watching it all with the comfort of each other's company.

But, robbed of that hope like a slap in the face, I'd never felt so alone and so scared.

The queue as we left the bus twenty minutes later was something else. From above, it would have looked like a gigantic, crowded colony of ants. But, finally, to my relief, within the mile-long queue of distraught people who'd been separated from people they knew, I actually laid eyes on someone I had known for years.

I knew there would be. There had to be. There were so many people around me that came from the same place I did. Same town, same district. Don't get me wrong, people from outside the town were there, too, but I just had to wait patiently for the numerous hours it took to get through the waiting bay so I could confirm what my eyes had seen.

In the meantime, I was thankful for the yellow railings that lined beside us to keep us all in form. They stood the perfect height for me to lean on through the weight of my impatience and laziness.

It took two hours before the queue had cut in half, and I found myself standing right next to the world's largest taxi. It was daunting.

Titan1 just had to be the single biggest thing I'd ever seen in my eighteen years alive. A single bolt or rivet that would join the panels to the supports, carried the dimensions of a bus wheel. I didn't even know they made bolts that massive.

You know when you join two solid objects together and you get a seam down the middle? With metal, they weld that seam shut. Well, a single welded seam on Titan1 ran what looked to be forty continuous feet between two gargantuan panels. The weld itself sat as thick as a plank of pallet wood. The panels they joined still stunk of the glossy green-hue pain that decorated them. It smelled like a freshly painted radiator. In fact, I'm pretty sure our house held the same whiff when my Mum would re-decorate the door frames as part of her 'spring clean' routine. I could still hear it now...

"Don't you touch that bloody frame!" she'd yell above everything else. "I've just painted it!"

Some things you just never know how much you'll miss until you do, and as I stood next to this... spectacle of a spaceship, I couldn't help but let my mind drift off into the unknown.

I don't know how long I stood there, but it was long enough that the bag on my back weighed twice what it once did. I can't even remember moving down the line as people boarded, but eventually, I was standing at the entrance myself.

I trod the twenty-eight steps up into the lower floor of Titan1, after the stiff, stressed, uniformed woman stamped the crumpled ticket that had sat in my wallet for six months. She looked like she was underpaid. Though, where would she have spent any she did get paid? Vending machines aboard the Titan? Oh, I did hope there were vending machines. Regardless, she needed to lighten up a little. She wasn't the only one going through perhaps their roughest day ever. Everybody whose ticket she stamped felt the exact same stress. Besides, she was getting a ride out of there, too. She didn't even need a ticket. Her ticket was her job – all the volunteer staff for the boarding, all officials and all Initiative suits were guaranteed a space on the Titans, without a ticket. That's just the start of a long list of questionable choices made by the stuck-up representatives that ran the whole thing.

"Noddy," I heard someone shout as I slung the bag from my back into a storage locker I was directed to.

I recognised the voice… it matched a face I'd seen whilst queuing. And as I turned around, there he was.

My friend, Toby. He pushed his way through a crowd of panicking passengers just to say hello to me.

He looked like he'd just woken up. No surprise there, Toby had never woken up for anything on time in the years I'd known him. He always ran late for something. From what I recall, all he had strewn across his shoulder, was the backpack he used to carry to college. The same battered crosshatch design, the same missing left strap. Considering we left college seven months ago, I was shocked that the bag still had even an ounce of life left in it. Even back then it looked like its days were numbered.

It sat on a diagonal, from his left shoulder to the right of his ribs, just how he always wore it. I'll admit, I was a little thrown off when he hugged me. More so by the curls of his brown hair as they tickled my nose. I always wondered what I'd look like with hair like his, but I was so used to the safe style I always defaulted to: short back and sides, with enough growth on top that I could flick my dark fringe from left to right. I like it, basic as it is.

"Dude," Toby said. "Can you believe this is happening?"

I couldn't. I could read the loss and confusion in his eyes like it was written in bold. The same that filled mine. As my breath shook with the quiver of my body, I hugged him back. God knows I needed it. It was that or hug the kind-faced lady that directed me to the lockers… because that would have gone down well…

I looked at Toby as he removed his hug and faced me.

"Thank God you're here," I told him. "I was worried I'd have nobody to talk to."

"Where's Emily?"

I told him the news. That she wasn't headed for Titan1, rather the blue-tinted ship that sat nearly forty miles from where we stood. My short bus ride was nothing compared to what hers would have been, and they both left from the same town.

Even though I'd not seen him since we went our separate ways after college, it was a blessing that Toby was there. I thought of how we could catch up, report life changes, and reminisce. Everything. Time would fly on Titan1, at least, that was what I thought his presence there meant.

We followed the kind-faced woman to the seventh floor. I call her that because I was too busy staring at her face than the nametag on her chest.

It was hard to lose sight of her in the massive ship. Her high visibility jacket made her stand out like the moon at midnight. Me and Toby stuck to each other's sides like glue, both thankful that we were syncing our footsteps with someone who wasn't a stranger.

Through that moment, it felt like only yesterday that we were kicking that football up and down Hank's abandoned mill on Bakersfield Close. I won't lie, I missed that mill as much as I already missed home, for a few reasons.

I can't begin to explain what met me when we arrived with a crowd of others on floor number seven. A vast mirrored row of… incubators it looked like. An infinite row of silver pods with glass doors that were all perched open in wait, like an invitation. Maybe it was my moderately lazy eye, but I had to steal a second glance at the sci-fi heaven before me.

They beeped in pattern as the small monitors that hung above them flashed yellow and red with readings I couldn't begin to understand. I don't know what it all meant, but it looked awesome. It was like I'd stepped into the future. Oh, how the irony of that sentence is *not* lost on me.

My tongue twitched as I tasted the sterilisers the pods had been wiped down with. The scent mixed with the air like an invasive perfume. The cute guide pointed at one, then told me I'd have to get in it 'soon.' Even now, I know that wasn't on the forms. I remember exactly what was on them as my heart bled ink into the pages before Nan and Grandad.

SANCTUARY ABOARD TITAN1

BEDS AND RESOURCES WILL BE PROVIDED

ACTIVITIES AND NIGHTLIFE

WE'RE A BUNCH OF LIARS

Okay, maybe that last one wasn't on there, but it may as well have been… because they'd lied through and through. The evidence lay right in front of me and announced itself with every beep and flash of its monitor.

I would say I turned to look at the guide, but in honesty, my eyes never left her for long. Red hair, hazel eyes… a weakness of mine. I'm only human, after all.

I asked her, "What does it do?"

She beat around the bush so hard that her brown eyes looked as lost as mine. Something about sleeping, something else about hyper… something. She saw my mind escape into theatricals, so she dumbed it down for me.

"It's a time capsule for people."

Now that… that had stolen my attention. It looked super cool, even Toby thought the same. It was like something from Star Trek, but we were living it. As proud nerds, we approved.

For an hour, I think, me and Toby, both technically 'adults,' re-enacted our favourite moments from Star Trek movies and episodes. The space around us practically begged for it.

We pretended the pods contained alien life from distant planets – we had to protect them at all costs from an invasion of evil forces hell-bent on genocide. But then, Miss 'good-looking buzzkill' ruined the moment as she spoke through a speakerphone that pointed right at us. It was time to 'mount.'

I'm not sure if she was from where we were, but that definitely meant something else to me and Toby. The silent laugh we shared reinforced that.

Her head turned to the pods that me and Toby were messing with, and she just stared us down without a single blink. I guess it was time to get in.

We did, with caution as we took our shoes off and placed them on the shelf that sat underneath. The pods were the epitome of awesome when we were outside them, but as we lay inside, that feeling ran dry quicker than isopropyl alcohol.

"We'll wake you when it's time," she said. It was a gentle voice. It soothed me enough that I didn't immediately try and escape as she slid the glass panel across. That would have certainly been my reaction otherwise.

"Slow breaths."

I think that's what she said. Once that panel clicked into place, exterior sounds became a series of mumbles, like my ears had been submerged in deep waters all of a sudden.

The inside began to fill with white vapour that admittedly, scared me for a moment. It was really cold. I'd seen warmer days fishing with my dad in the winter at Frank's Pond.

As the mist did whatever it was there to do, I read the small label on the underside of the glass panel above me.

WARNING

IN THE EVENT OF MALFUNCTION

PULL YELLOW CORD

My limbs became numb, My eyes closed.

I felt like I'd been struck by an avalanche that had pinned me down whilst it engulfed me For a moment, my skin burned from underneath, starting with my face, until eventually it too, became numb.

That's the last thing I remember before the same calm voice spoke to me…

When it woke me.

"Two things are infinite: the universe and human stupidity; and I'm not so sure about the universe."

- Albert Einstein

ENTRY 3
INFORMATION OVERLOAD

It was a muffle, but it disturbed me. Was it me who was distorted, or she?

I'd almost forgotten where I was. Woken from my slumber where I dreamt of home and convinced myself that it was reality, and Titan1 was the nightmare. But the twist of my gut as I stirred in the pod stole that light from me.

It felt like I was a patient, waking from a heavy anaesthetic, discombobulated while I limply chased thoughts that roamed infinite circles inside my lead-heavy head.

I can't say what it was with accuracy, but as the glass panel of the pod slid to my right, I couldn't move my body. I could feel it, sure… just about. But I couldn't move it. Like my motor function had fizzled out… lost signal. Head to toe, it felt like I'd spent a millennium sleeping in the snow.

"It's alright," a soft voice said to me as I started to sit. I'd recognised it pretty quickly as the one paired with red hair and nice eyes.

"It'll take some time to adjust. You've been in there… a little while."

How long was a while? And where was Toby? I looked to my right.

He was two pods away from me, suffering the same disorientation. Like a kitten chasing a laser pointer, he flung his hands about in all directions.

When my movement came back, and eventually it did, I lifted my legs over the side of the pod and let them dangle six inches from the ground. Only then, was when I saw the yellow cord the label noted. Right under the crease of my legs as they bent over the ledge. You'd think they'd have made it obvious considering it was a deterrent to a 'malfunction.'

The air tingled my feet as it slipped through my toes, and I couldn't remember if it was me, or someone else who'd taken my shoes off. That's how clouded my brain was. It looked at the world through heavily frosted glass.

It all served to confuse me. Even my eyes took time to adjust. For what felt like the longest time, I looked upon the floor filled with pods in an overexposure that wrapped everything in a gaussian blur.

"How long have I been in there?" I wondered. It felt like a normal sleep I'd have nightly at home, but I never recalled feeling drugged to my teeth after a long night's rest. It was… a high. Hallucinatory.

It took three days to make sense of the information the suits had fed us all over the tannoy system. Almost as long as it took to keep any of the rationed food down whilst my stomach settled back into reality. A day less than it took for my awkward feet to remember how to walk in a simple straight line without buckling under the forgotten weight of my twelve stone body.

My slumber was a fraction longer than I'd guessed. 153 years longer, to be precise. A number that threw my brain at lightspeed into a collision with my barely-together skull.

It would have been May 19th, just four days later.

Imagine 153 years and a couple of months separating your 18th and 19th birthdays. I'll let you calculate the math of how old that really made me.

Toby had taken to life on the ship like a bird to a fountain inside the three days It had taken me to rebalance. He loved it, in fact. I hadn't seen him much during my adjustment days, just the mid-forties parents that struggled with me, who fretted because some of their children had boarded Titan4 instead. Some of them refused to believe how long it had been since we entered the pods, just like myself.

There was this one man among them, Philip, his name was. He kept checking in on me every few hours. Just to make sure I was doing alright with it all. I liked him; he reminded me of my dad. Stocky, a thick beard my child-like face could only ever dream of, and the constant deceptive look of middle-aged grump that dressed his kind face.

His son, Tobias if I remember right, had been boarded on Titan4. It turned out that the government bastards that wrote their invitations sent two tickets to his house, for him and his son, each with a different boarding location. They knew they lived together, and knew they were father and son. What struck me down was when Philip told me how old Tobias was.

Six. Six years old. Philip had tried to argue his case for months, but nobody listened. Instead, he was sent a caution. Either they abided by their printed instructions, or they relinquish the rights to their tickets. It was sycophantic and barbaric.

Nothing surprised me at that point. Something just screamed 'corruption' about the people who orchestrated the initiative. As I said, it was a long list of questionable choices, and it only got longer. Not that we could do anything about it, but it was *nice and convenient* how they all got their places aboard the Titans.

Even the secretary of the initiative, Sylvia Therman got her own nice and cosy room on Titan3. It might not sound so strange at first, but what you need to know is Sylvia was in her seventies when boarding day unfortunately arrived. She'd been around forever. When the plans to unite and build the ships were put into motion, Sylvia was already above the age threshold they'd go on to announce as unfit to board. Sylvia and her cronies ruled out my grandparents, even though my nan, was three years younger than she.

Funny how an exception comes to pass when you're one of the scumbags leading the operation, isn't it?

She wasn't the only one either. Aboard Titan1 alone, right on the highest floor where the cabinet and pilot decks were, a select few 'officials' had passed the 'below 50's' barrier by an easy decade or three. And yet... us, the pathetic lower-class humans that leaned on them for survival, well, we had separate rules. Rules vastly different to theirs.

I got to know Philip and the people around me pretty well. He, Toby and Suzie, a woman Philip had taken a keen eye for, even made me a birthday cake from their pudding rations. We shared it around as many as we could, and for a single day, everything felt less… caged off from reality. With people like that around me, the weeks that came to pass drifted by a lot quicker than I imagined they would.

Ten days later, we got the announcement that none of us expected. Me and Toby were kicking a ball up and down the pod aisle on our floor. We'd made it from collected ration-pack paper bundled together with whatever sticky tape we could find. Some duct tape, some clear tape and even some masking tape. It worked pretty well, and we were having fun until the screech of the tannoys kicked in and startled us both. Right in the middle of a tied game of penalty shootout.

The stranger who shouted from the heavens told us that in four short weeks, we'd be descending on earth.

A planet that, to us, we'd only just left yet missed so dearly at the same time. The lingering thought in many heads around me, including my own, was how much it had changed in the apparent century and a half we'd been away from it.

My grandparents, friends that remained there, and families that chose to stay behind, would all be gone, in what, to me, was a simple sleep and ten days in space.

In what I barely even remember, through the anxiety that stamped through my system like a mob of cattle, four weeks soon came to pass. Though, 32 days was closer to five weeks than it was four.

Thursday. At least somehow, it felt like one. I looked from the bay windows of Titan1 and the first thing I was greeted with was the moon. Closer than I'd ever seen it before. It didn't glow as much as it does when you look at it from the ground at night. It was just this grey, cratered ball of rock that floated there in isolation. I could literally see into the canyons and imperfections on the surface as though I was standing on it. It wasn't near as smooth as it was always depicted to be through photographs and art.

And there it was. Right behind it, as the moon began to shift away and revealed it as though it was a sly secret.

Home. Earth.

A planet that six weeks ago, as far as I was concerned, I was standing on firm-footed. It looked desaturated; void of the colourfulness that made it stand out from the rest of our solar system. Most of the bright, vivid blue that shone from its oceans and seas had become a dreary grey with smears of brown and green.

Some of the blue remained, where the deepest, largest bodies of water lay, but it was clear to me that whatever happened in my absent years aboard the ship, had dried up the planet on a level unseen, and it scared me.

The cracks and imperfections that scarred it, courtesy of storms and earthquakes, came into view. My body trembled more and more the closer we got. Over the hours it took, the more beaten and dry it looked.

"Safe to return," they said in their announcement just weeks before. "The moment we've all been waiting for."

It didn't look safe to me. Not up close like that.

I'd never seen the sprinkle of dark hair on my arms stand so tall. The goosebumps, sure. I remember how they used to freak me out as a child. Like running your hand over microscopic bubble wrap. But my hairs reaching for the stars? That was new, but I knew what spurred it; they stood the moment the anxiety-filled adrenaline pumped through me.

Then we landed. As soft as anything. To most of us, it felt like we were still in the skies, despite what the view from the windows told us. But there it was, the same place I remember drowning in boredom during the wait. The same yellow bollards and rails that kept the queue in order, only they weren't so yellow anymore. In fact, everything that looked the same, also didn.t.

"In a formerly line!" the officials shouted as thousands of eager and lost civilians rushed from the massive doors of Titan1. I should know, I was one of them, and I didn't plan on sticking around.

Sorry, Philip. Sorry, Toby and Suzie, but I had a home to return to. Even if they were my neighbours and my friends. Even if I had spent a century and a half with them, I had my own space back. A space I missed. One I wasn't going to pretend didn't exist.

I took no time at all escaping the clutches of the 'arrival control,' that were first to disembark as I ducked and weaved through the crowd. Funny, how they thought they were our leaders.

The bucket list in my head had but two words in it…

Jupiter Avenue.

"I sat in the dark and thought: There's no big apocalypse. Just an endless procession of little ones."

- Neil Gasman

"Apocalypse has come and gone. We're just grubbing in the ashes."

- Samuel R. Delan

ENTRY 3.5
THE BENCH

So, now that I've filled you in, that leaves me right back where we started. Figured I'd hash out the details in the hope it would make a little more sense down the line. Sense is something that's been missing from everything as of late.

Now, I'm sitting, talking directly to you upon a half-disfigured stone bench at the base of what used to be a statue of our once mayor, Roland Keen. It's slapped right in the middle of what used to be the busiest roundabout in town.

Now, it's just as alone as the rest of it, and a sad irony lies upon the plaque rested on Roland's statue. Words that now seem like lies.

ROLAND OF WENTON

A TOWN FOUNDED IN 1846

MAY IT LIVE A LONG AND PROSPEROUS LIFE

AND OUTLIVE THE WORLD IT HAS GRACED

D – RAINER EST. 2003

It took me no longer than thirty minutes to get here as I ran from Titan1 and their whole 'formerly line' debacle.

Who were they kidding? Everyone aboard that floating goliath was eager to return to what was snatched from them. 'Formerly line.' Piss off.

Anyway, I think it took about thirty or forty minutes, I don't know for sure. My phone hasn't left my bag. It's in there with some scrap journals, science books I've been stealing relevant quotes from, and my pencil case, and it's had no charge in it since I woke up. I guess 153 years is enough to drain a battery, and I'd be lucky to find a working outlet here. Hence, I turned to the paper I had stashed in my bag, and I started this journal.

There's literally nothing else to do…

I can't help but wonder, you know? Does time even work the same anymore? It's basically a rebirth zone now, here in this little corner of space we called home. I'm pretty sure the time we'd tracked, ended when we left in 2024 … so we start again from zero? Who's to decide?

My original plan was to head home, and that's still the case now, but there are a few more places on my list now. Places that even stepping foot back here, reminded me of. I think I'll do my thing, go, and explore what was taken from me, and, if it doesn't hurt too much, I'll write it down.

I've been sitting on this crooked bench for too long now, writing what you've already read in the first entries. I'd almost forgotten I was back here. But the roundabout that served my peace is sitting just a hundred meters from a turning I've craved to lean my head around.

Now, it's time for me to take another walk, but I'll pick this back up later and tell you all about it if I have the energy to.

"Home isn't the four walls around you. It's not the street you live on, but it's the people. Your friends and your family. If you miss them when they're gone, they were home."

- Willow Sawyer, Mum.

ENTRY 4
JUPITER AVENUE

As promised, consider it 'picked back up.'

More moss and overgrowth, than concrete and brick, was Jupiter Avenue as my head peered around the junction. I remember how it used to look like it was yesterday, again, because, to me, it really wasn't too long ago. The passage of time really took its toll on me.

But I was home. Finally.

The kerbs still lifted where I remembered. The same ones I'd bounce the football off with my friends on a Saturday afternoon. The same ones I slipped off at seven years old. My mum always said it looked like a shark's tooth, the pointed scar it left on my right knee. She wasn't wrong.

Exactly 107 steps it took, just as it always did when I'd get off the bus at the top of the road. A game I'd made up in the boredom of the walk. But that's how many steps it took to get from the bus stop to the gate of my family home, where I stood.

NUMBER 37

It wasn't there anymore, the gate. My best guess is that the bolts snapped off when the rust took it over. It was leaning in a lifeless slouch up against the short wall that separated our garden from the one next door, the same one I used to park my scooter against as a child. I couldn't even kick the gate open until it sprung back into place and slid its rocker into the latch. Another thing I used to do. I always did get told off for it, not that it ever stopped me.

I traipsed the slabs I'd walked when I said goodbye to my grandparents, minding the cracks… superstitious as I was. We'd had enough bad luck already, buckets of it. I never remembered the challenge being that tough though; there were more cracks these days.

The door to the house was open as I approached it. By open, I mean the wood had rotted away until all that remained, was the solid beam that ran the length of it and strapped the hinges to the frame. Even then it still struggled to hold on.

The wooden steps before it, that my dad built to replace the old ones, were rotted too. They bowed and shifted under my feet as I walked over them. It felt like a thin dock on unstable waters.

My head spun in every direction it could find when I stared blindly down the entrance hall. It was only ever ten feet long and four feet wide, but, somehow, now it felt bigger.

Once coated in a grey and silver floral wallpaper than my mum and nan spent two whole days fitting. Once littered with my brother's countless medals, slung on nails that my dad battered into the wall, proud and relishing in a flood of sporting talent that never passed down to me.

Now, the hall was stained by the century of weather that had attacked it. The wallpaper dropped, robbed of colour, and the parts of it that remained glued to the wall were done so by the moss that climbed them. And that was just the opening stretch that led from the main door to the kitchen.

It was a pitiful corpse of what raised me, yet, somehow, it still felt like home. I'd stretch far enough to say I wouldn't *not* feel like home to me. It's exactly why I went back.

The smell that punched me in the face as I scaled the broken, uneasy staircase was ghastly. Rotting wood infused with mould and moss. Rainwater trapped in the air pockets that textured the walls and withered hundred-year-old carpets. If the doom of humanity had a smell, I'd stumbled upon it, and it carried through the house.

Past the main bedroom that had collapsed with the corner of the building where beams had weakened and caved. Past the bathroom that now housed half of the slate tiles that had sunken in from the roof. And through to a room that once upon a time, I never wanted to leave.

My room. My self-made sanctuary.

The bed was still there. Well, the metal frame of it was, anyway, despite the rust and blatant fractures that riddled it. Tucked in the corner with barely enough room to open the door more than halfway. I'm a skinny guy. I always have been, so that never bothered me. Who says you can't fit a double bed in a single room?

Besides, whenever I was in trouble with my dad… he was a pretty stocky guy, so he could never chase me further than my door. Consider it my own security barrier.

Some springs and cloth lay around it in a mess, so either my mattress decomposed with half of the house, or someone had lifted off with it.

Well, I suppose if they were still here, still on the ground, they needed it more than I did. For all I knew, they borrowed my room, but no such evidence was there. It just looked abandoned, baited to the storms that thrashed it.

Everything but the frame of the bed was… soft. Rotted and damp, stained with the same stench that ran throughout the entire building. The floor beneath me dented deeper as I trod it, so much that I would have held more faith in the puddled grass that lined the stretch of the garden below.

The urge to perch on my bed was as strong as it ever was whenever I'd stepped into my room. But I took a solid pass on sitting near anything in the vicinity this time. All the things I'd remembered were disintegrated into a soggy mess that only reminded me of the disaster that struck there.

I did find one of my old die-cast trains though. My dad loved them, I kept a few lined on the windowsill after we lost him. They sat right next to some framed pictures of him and my mum. The pictures themselves were ruined. Faded, as though someone had erased them, and it made me feel sick.

The train I picked up was covered entirely in rust. It was nothing but a furry, cracked, and orange variant of its former self. Though, at this point weren't we all? I wiped as much of it as I could on the disgusting carpet and chucked it in the front pocket of my bag.

I wish I could have stayed there. I never knew it would be so… inhabitable. More fool me. But I also couldn't leave without a final look around.

Downstairs… The dining table where I signed the boarding papers. I could still see my nan and grandad there as they watched me. The now beaten units across the back wall where my mum kept my nan's China crockery sets. The counter on the right that hooked around above the appliances, slouched in a dead mass on the rotted tile floor. Nothing was as I remembered it. It all felt like a twisted rendition of it all that had been handed to me by the devil.

"Here," said Satan, as he handed me a silver platter. "For old time's sake." Then I'd look upon the tray to find two lumps of coal and a broken home. In my head, that's exactly what had happened.

"One day," I thought to myself as I dropped my shoulders with the thought. "One day soon, I'll come back here and rebuild."

The others from Titan1 could do whatever they wanted, whether that be to follow the commands of liars or make something of their own.

But all I wanted, was my old life back. I wanted the Saturday afternoons playing football. I wanted the greetings from my mum and dad when I walked through the door, whether it be a telling off for something I definitely did, or a 'how was school?'

And I'd give anything for that.

"We don't live forever, Ned. None of us. Make your mark and make one nobody else can follow. You don't need medals for us to be proud of you."

- Benjamin Sawyer, Dad

ENTRY 5
ST. PETER'S

I was sat, for what may as well have been another full turn of the planet beneath me, and I just… stared. Ogled, even. Right in front of my wide eyes, stood two identical headstones made from black marble, that I'd seen so many times before. White streaks decorated them not unlike streams of smoke and helped them stand out from the rotted crowd that surrounded them.

Mossy, just like everything else. It took the shine away from that which once graced each stone. Now they were dull and weathered, partnered with the scenery around them. I could barely make out the names that once labelled them in prominence, elegant in the gold lettering. It took a firm wipe from the cuff of my jacket to peel off the first, thick layer of growth, dust, and age.

They still weren't perfect, but at least I could see the writing.

BENJAMIN HARRISON SAWYER

FATHER, SON, BROTHER

WILLOW MAY-ANNE SAWYER

MOTHER, DAUGHTER, SISTER

My parents.

It had been… at least in the flow of time that I remembered, only six weeks since I last saw the grounds of St. Peter's cemetery. The day before I boarded Titan1. Only then, flowers were present in colourful bloom, the grass was neat-cut and the stones and decorations that lined those lost were clean and well-presented. The stones were polished.

As I looked blankly at the headstones ahead of me, the passage of time sunk in a little bit more. I'd always polished them, every chance I got. Always took new flowers every time I visited. Considering it was a fifteen-minute walk from our home on Jupiter Avenue, I made it a habit of mine. After all, they didn't like a messy house, so why would they like their place of rest to be a mess? Even without that sentiment, these two people raised me. They did everything for me, with no questions. There was no way on this curse of a planet I would have let it get untidy.

I never told you, did I? I probably scanned over it instead. Impulse, because I don't really like to talk about it.

I lost them a year ago… I guess to be accurate, it was 154 years ago now. Nevertheless, I still remember what was said to me as I sat at that table in our kitchen as if it was just five minutes ago.

They'd travelled to Santa Monica as they did every year without fail; Mum was obsessed with the pier. Her father who passed years ago used to hold the same tradition every summer when she was a child. I guess she just followed suit and fell in love with the world he'd introduced her to. I never bothered to go with them on their holidays, it was always the quietest eight days of the year where I'd have the house to myself and could get away with pretty much anything, to a degree. Parties for the few people that would show. I never had to tidy my room until that final day when they'd text me when they were at the airport.

I fell in love with the freedom of it all. More so as I got older. Only the last time they took their holiday, all it took was four days until my grandparents knocked on the door.

Mum and Dad were gone, they told me. No goodbye, no warning, just… gone. A tsunami had rocked the North Pacific. You'd be mistaken to think they were but two of an unlucky few, but in reality, the tsunami that struck them was one of the biggest that had ever been recorded. It was all over the news. Long Beach, Santa Monica, Westwood, and everything in between, were all wiped out in minutes because Earth shook and created a monumental wave.

"Don't come back," was the last thing I said to my parents.

I was only joking, of course, a jab at the peace I'd be left in as they trotted the globe. But those few words that slipped my tongue haunted me for months after. It was then that my grandparents sold their bungalow and moved to Jupiter Avenue. They took over the home. All in a selfless awareness that I wouldn't want to leave it.

A home that was once theirs, now theirs again, through events they'd trade their own lives to prevent.

Every tsunami report that echoed through the news channels from that moment on, took me right back to seeing Nan and Grandad fall into their own chests as they broke the news to me over a cup of tea and some chocolate digestives.

They were the only two people I had left after that. Of course, I had my friends, but that was different. Home felt lonely and broken. To wake up and not be able to smell the cheap aftershave my dad used to wear, not able to hear my mum hum to the songs on the radio as she curled her hair. It felt as lonely as the world does now, maybe even more.

What makes it worse now, is that those two people, my grandparents, to the ache of my heart, weren't graced with a resting place like my parents were. They shared a different fate. Two heroes who faced earth's tantrum head-on, whilst I was thousands of miles away from the planet, sleeping safe, oblivious to what they'd go on to endure.

They had nothing to show for the mass of bravery within them, except what I held inside my own head with the memories of their unconditional love and support. It only angered me more, the knowledge that a government that swore to protect us, shunned my two angels, and labelled them weak when in actual fact, they were the strongest of us all.

As the tears dripped down my face at St. Peter's, like rain off a canopy, I made a promise to my parents.

"I'll rebuild it all," I said, echoing what I'd once said in my exploration of the house. The words that left my mouth clashed with the wind that bit away at my ears.

"I'll protect our home, just like you did."

Then with a clenched grasp, I ripped the shaggy, wet grass from its roots before their headstones, so my two idols could watch by in undisturbed clarity whilst I started anew. They were the two people who introduced me to the world, and so by default, they were the two I'd chosen to guide me through what came next, even if it was just replaying their life-lessons as I stumbled my way through a now uncertain future.

I was aware that I couldn't stick around forever, even though I wanted to. The pain of seeing them, given the context of it all, was… rough. It spun my brain with a velocity so dense it practically gave me vertigo.

I didn't know where I was headed next, at first, but I just had this sinking feeling that everything surrounding me, no matter where I went, was on a mission to pull away at my soul until nothing at all remained. To rip it clean from inside me and watch as I'd buckle and beg for it back with worthless, meaningless prayers.

That… unfortunately was what life was to be now, it felt like. A never-ending downward wind of depressive episodes, let-downs, and harsh realisations. Memories of what once was that would antagonise me like a playground bully high on the pain it birthed inside me.

To say I was deeply ashamed of myself for ever signing that boarding pass, was a massive understatement. Even if it was the right thing to do.

"The distinction between the past, present and future is only a stubbornly persistent illusion."

- Albert Einstein

ENTRY 6
STOOD AT THE GATES

Just on the other side of our small yet always busy town. That's where it sat, lonely, beaten, and victim to the time that had passed since I'd last laid eyes on it. It's where I spent a full two years making new friends.

Most people would have called it a college, but I called it a second home. Once teeming with eager life, now barely clinging to its own. As much as my home was what made me who I am, the people I met there, at Tilston Grange Academy, and the college itself, played as big a part in that as my parents did.

It was the place I was most thankful to know when the world took Mum and Dad from me. It's where Toby was, where Sasha and Emily were. I could name a bunch of them, but those few, I spent most of my time with, especially Emily. We were thrilled when we were all accepted in.

Me and Emily grew up in the same schools together since nursery, and Toby moved from Ireland and came here to live, then became our friend a little later, in year ten. Many others I grew up with got accepted there too, it's where most of us went. Hannah, Graham, Steve, the list goes on, but you'd have no idea who they all were. Even to me, they just became familiar faces.

I couldn't get inside the grounds, as I stood and stared from the gates. A six-foot glossed green cast-iron barricade that even my mum could have climbed over. But it wasn't that which stopped me. The buildings I'd spent multiple terms in, studying Computer Science, with no idea what I was being told… no wonder I failed. Four floors and I was forever on the third; a floor which was met by the fourth and second now in a slanted lean, like a rotten sandwich of concrete and wood. I wouldn't put it past it smelling like my old home these days.

Those around it were all in the same condition. That's the problem with most brick-and-mortar buildings, they don't last forever. The big 'B-block' building where some of us would struggle with extra math and literature classes, was just a brisk wind away from meeting the ground it was built on. I didn't go back to have my body splattered by the same building that once had the same effect on my mind. So, to remember from safety was my aim.

Despite what was right in front of me, it still reminded me of happier times. Like a projector on a cladded wall, the memories played out in front of me. For a moment, for a brief shutting out of the chaos that swam around me, I smiled and let them play.

I pictured the courtyard that sat on the rear of B-block. Where we'd play football. Me, Toby, and Emily with a few others we all knew. Goalposts were painted into the bricks because they couldn't afford physical ones, it made for a great game of dodge when you blasted the ball at the keeper, usually Toby, and it rebounded off the wall at rocket speed. I could still see the tatty football Toby would bring in his battered bag. Its hexagonal padding would tear from the seams with every kick, and they would flap in the wind. If you listened carefully, you could hear the ball vibrate as it spun.

On the other side of the court, was one of the two fields. We tried kicking the ball on that particular one once, but with no wall to stop the easy goals past Toby, it just sailed for miles. The kicker would have to chase it unless the kicker was Emily, then she'd bat her eyes at me.

"Can you get it for me, please?" she'd beg, knowing I wouldn't say no.

But on the other side of that field, right before a little woodland area that a lot of the smokers used to sneak into, there was a bench. A long, green-painted bench that could seat four. It was the very bench Emily would sit at and tuck into her favoured hash brown sandwich she'd grab from the canteen. She was always odd with her food, but one day she tore me a bit of it off and asked me to try it.

I'll tell you now that it wasn't even that bad. Like a chip butty… but fluffy. We'd always sit at lunch and talk about college and what would come next whilst we ate. How Emily always wanted to move on after it all and find something in the Navy; a place where her uncle held a position as a pilot since she was just two years old. It never bothered her how long he would be away, she just knew he was a hero, and that's all she really ever focused on.

"Yeah, me too," I'd say when what I really meant was to praise her.

I could never see past the part-time retail job she'd helped me get at the time. Seventeen years old working shelves in a supermarket, but it paid me on the days I wasn't in college.

The bike shed to the right of the entrance gates I was standing at, was practically non-existent. A Perspex curve that hugged a metal frame, like something of a fancy bus shelter, with a row of metal rails poking from the bottom that you'd lock your wheels into. I almost lost count of how many bikes went missing from there in the two years I attended.

We'd all hide behind it, like it wasn't almost completely see-through, and have a cigarette here and there. Kids will do what kids will do I guess, but neither me nor Emily were actually smoking them. We just pretended… like we thought it was cool. It was all as innocent as doing that could be, minus the fact that the cigarettes were those which Graham had pinched from his Mum's packet. The thing I missed most about that bike shed, was the conversations pre-lesson at near-nine in the morning. Bragging about skills on FIFA and betting odds against beating each other. Even Emily joined in, but as much as none of us admitted it, we were all scared of betting against her; she was better than any of us at it.

Seriously, I played a game with her at my house one afternoon on a weekend. She'd nipped round to escape her boredom and make something of an empty day. I had a second controller, so I fired up a game. She beat me 6-0. And I considered myself fairly good at it, too. It wasn't beginners' luck, or a fluke, either.

Between me and this paper… we played four matches that day. I lost every single one of them.

There were never enough words in existence to showcase just how much the college and the people there meant to me, so I'd written this entry to tell whoever may read it just how badly I wanted all of it back.

The innocence of it all and the natural path of life as we all learned our places in life and grew up. It will never be like that again. At least, not in my lifetime anyway. What I'm trying, and failing to say, is that the longer I looked around and remembered the world I'd lived in before the confusion and the destruction, the more I realised I'd taken it all for granted. I'd drifted my way through my job in limp mode and I'd chosen laziness over productivity every single day of the week.

I could feel in my bones as I stood at those gates, just how foolish I'd been, for never understanding how sacred our time was. If anything, it made me want it all back even more, so I could do it all differently.

I needed a break from it all. An escape, even. So, I made my way to another place I could never forget.

A place where my thoughts could escape into the clouds, almost literally. A place I'd only mentioned briefly in a previous entry.

"Closing your eyes isn't going to change anything. Nothing's going to disappear just because you can't see what's going on. In fact, things will be even worse the next time you open your eyes. That's the kind of world we live in. Keep your eyes wide open. Only a coward closes his eyes. Closing your eyes and plugging your ears won't make time stand still."

- Haruki Murakami

ENTRY 7
HOLD THEM TIGHT, THE MEMORIES

Just like I always did when I wanted to clear my head or escape from something, I found myself on the roof of Hank's abandoned mill in Bakersfield Close downtown. In the same place that me, Toby, and Emily would kick the football about on lonely weekends or early college finishes when we weren't ready to go home and see the day out. The inside was big enough for a small game, so that's what we did.

It may have been another lengthy walk, but it was worth it. It was already deserted for the longest time, years before I left, but seeing it riddled with green and dishevelled only highlighted just how much time had passed.

Even there, where I always sat on the roof, it felt like a complete stranger to me.

It took more effort than it usually would to climb to the top; I had to dodge piles of the ceilings that had collapsed through the floors. Like a fat cat, stairs became somewhat of an issue for me. The mill had four flights of them, then an extended flight to the left of the top floor that led you to a forever-open wooden door that opened up on the roof.

The door wasn't there anymore, as was the case with most things wooden. Evidently, wood doesn't last a lifetime before it cripples and rots through weather and loneliness.

It all took me to my favourite seat in the town, right at the corner of the building. Don't worry though, I wasn't a fool who'd test life and death at the top of a multi-storey building. There was a small lip that ran around the entire roof, about three feet from the edge and stood about the same in height. I sat on that; I always did. I just let the thoughts flow through me, and like enemy gates opening, they pushed to the front immediately. No patience or second-guessing, just a stampede.

I remembered the first time I took Emily to my sacred place. How her silky blonde hair would flap about as the wind circled the building. We talked so much as we sat there. So much, Mum would often call me out of worry because I'd lose track of time.

As I sat there, alone in a beaten world, one particular day came back to me as if it was as recent as the last breath I took. The day Emily told me she 'really needed to talk.'

Of course, if my friends need to talk, I'm 'all ears.' I looked deep into her ocean-blue eyes as she muttered the words. She wasn't shy about them, but I was. She told me she had a crush on my brother, Richard. As red-faced as it made me, I heard her out… that's what friends are for. Ah, how her heart broke more than even mine when we lost him.

Have I told you about Richard? I don't think I have. Maybe I should, the roof's as good a place as any to wear my heart on my sleeve.

Richard was four years older than me. His whole life was ahead of him and man, he was the best. The medals that lined the once-proud hallway of my home were all his… football-related for the most part.

He was an athlete, the guy whose football team hoped would be there on days they needed a win, or when the biggest game of the season was afoot. He didn't play the field though; he was the keeper. I don't think I ever saw Richie let one through in any of the games I watched as I grew up.

'The hands of god,' they called them - the game winners that sat attached to his wrists. Large palms, lanky fingers, and his six-foot-three stature made it almost impossible for anyone to score against him. I don't know where he got his height from, but I struggled to pass six feet tall.

When I was little, he'd pretend I was good at the same sport, and let a lousy penalty slip through in the garden, but I knew what he was doing. I always saw that ball roll in slow motion to those plastic, wind-vulnerable goalposts.

If he wasn't saving his football team – pun intended – he was running marathons. Whenever our small town got involved with the cities and towns that surrounded it and organised charity runs, he was straight on the computer. Within minutes of its announcement, he'd signed up, every single time, without fail, for seven years straight.

Six weeks of training would see Richie spend a little less time at home until the day of the event when he'd show up again with a medal in his hands. Another to line the wall of achievements our dad was ever so fond of.

We fought. All the time, as brothers do. After all, we egotistical buffoons only had each other to rally off growing up. I can still taste the pennies in my mouth from the day I took it too far and swung a kick so fast it swept me off my feet. I never realised how hard gravel was until my face met with it, to Richie's amusement.

Through his laughs, he'd help me back to my feet and ask if I was alright, but being a kid, I just told Mum that he did it. There was something so devilishly sweet about how his smile dropped whenever she told him off. Don't judge me, I was a lot smaller back then; a win was a win.

We lost him before we lost our parents. He took to a skiing trip in the alps with his football team. A trip with the boys as they celebrated their seasonal win during a break between college terms. A trip he never returned from.

That must run in the family, I guess.

Six long days of Mum worrying about him because she knew how dangerous skiing could be. Just as long as the amount of time my dad spent telling her that Richard was a big boy and how he could handle himself. In a way, he was right. The trip was fine, he'd had his fun, packed his bags, and began to make his way home. The text he sent, served to calm her.

HEADING FOR THE BUS

BE HOME SOON

LOVE YOU

A message that cursed him, I guess.

The bus that was sent to escort them from the lodge to the airport was what threatened him and his team when it veered off a narrow winding road, down an embankment and struck a tree. The driver, and 'Loco,' his friend, Lewis, also lost their lives that day with him.

The others were injured, but they managed to make it home in one piece. As my memory serves, twelve of them were on that bus, driver included. Nine made it home. A freak accident that changed our lives forever and sent a shockwave through the town.

As much as I always knew Richie was popular, I never realised *how* popular exactly, until after his tragic accident. The college held a remembrance ceremony for him where most of the students attended and lay flowers at the plaque that had been made for him and Loco. The funeral we held was packed full so much, that people had to stand down the skinny aisles of the church because there weren't enough seats to accommodate them all.

From that moment on, it felt like my whole life was defined by his loss. I don't think I even have to tell you how lonely the house felt without him in it. Nobody to argue with, playfight or worse, look up to. Just another reason to stay in my bedroom and shut the entire world out.

Like I said earlier, things keep changing. None of them ever for the better, it seems. Nineteen years of age now, and I'm pretty certain I'm the only remaining member of my beloved family. I don't know about distant relatives, uncles and aunts, cousins. I don't even know if my mum's mother is still out there, though I doubt it considering we celebrated her 70th birthday about five years ago.

This is the effect the roof has on you. It's often so quiet and relaxed that your mind picks what it wants to focus on. I could have easily told you that I had a brother called Richard and that we lost him a while ago, but instead, I lost myself in the memory. I'm not mad at it, when it comes to people I love, I'm grateful for the memories. Just as I am for the times that I shared with them before they were snatched away from me.

We all need a place like Hank's mill. Without one, who are we, and what are we doing? Life's too short to share it so often with people, and not remember how they made it better for you.

Without Richard, my social awkwardness would no doubt be stronger. Without my parents, I would never have made it so far. Without Emily, I would have struggled with school and definitely skipped on a chance at college. Without my grandparents, I would have lost myself numerous times over the years.

I dwell on the past because as my nan often pointed out to my mum, it's what made me. It's where I'm from, at the end of the day. And my future, well, so far that's not looking too great.

In honesty, I feel so messed up. I hold these memories of old in a fusion of those I hate but have to remember, and those I love and want to remember.

Welcome to life in 2177.

"Be careful where you focus your attention, kid. If you too heavily muster up a false state of comfort, it could be snatched away in a moment's notice."

- Grandad Sawyer

ENTRY 8
ADRIFT

I know I never said any of the memories I held were good, but to me, they all helped me focus on what was important, life.

I was accustomed to chaos, born into it and moulded by a lifetime of loss and destruction. If my return to this planet was a chance at redemption, the people I'd lost along the way were my guiding lights.

For the most part, it was all about remembering them, and them alone, so I guess these days it was just as fitting to sit on the roof and dwell on it all. My eyes would settle on the sky around me, often grey, sometimes clear, but always at peace with itself.

The tops of the buildings around me would peak through the bottom of my eye line as if to greet me with a shy 'hello.' The number of times in my years I'd sworn black and blue that I hated this town, only to sit on top of the mill and fall deeply in love with it, every time.

You can take the kid out of the town, but you can't take the town out of the kid. Or so they say, anyway. I get it now. But as I was saying… that small slice of solitude I found on the roof, I shared with Emily. We were so close we'd often be mistaken for a couple. Of course, we weren't, but when you're in your teenage years, two people of the opposite sex, and spend most of your time together, people would always and easily make something of it. Something from absolutely nothing.

But that's how we worked, me and Emily. Two people who grew up with each other from an early age and lived on opposite sides of a small town, yet somehow were still joined at the hip no matter what was thrown at us.

I think of her as a sister, almost. I always have, as anyone would if they were so close to her. I never actually had a sister, like I said, it was just me and Richie, but if I ever got to choose one it would be her. No hesitation and I always hoped she thought of me as a brother, but I always accepted 'best friend,' with open arms. That title was an award within itself if it came from her.

The roof did to me what it always did and veered my thoughts off in a random spray pattern until eventually, I sat there with the wonder of how she was doing on Titan4. Phones were out of the question; 153

years will render any battery useless. Even if they were charged, I'd bet good, yet worthless money on a signal being hard to find.

She did message me the day we boarded. A message I remember clearly, but I've chosen to keep to myself. The disappointment of us both boarding two separate ships still thrashed over me like it was a new revelation, a twisted nightmare once again dished out by the devil.

I know she would have chosen to take these steps with me down memory lane, through what once seemed like yesterday. She would have done exactly as I did and noted both the subtle and major differences in everything we saw. Her eye for detail was better than mine could ever be. If a stone was unturned, I'll tell you right now she'd know.

"Titan4 can't be far from landing," I thought as I sat there.

Its zone was on the other side of the city, granted, but I'd been on a Titan myself. You wouldn't miss one of those landings, even if it was a hundred or more miles away.

I hate to say it, but I really was struggling. I thought repeatedly for so many sleepless nights on Titan1 over the six weeks I waited to see my home again.

I thought about how I could go back to the house and pretend like none of it ever happened, and how I could walk Jupiter Street like it was just another walk back from the bus. But, with nobody to share it with, the house crippled… the town in pieces, empty and lonely, the two people I loved most already gone, and my grandparents now lost in the time I'd missed… I wondered if my hope was mistaken.

I was broken to pieces as the thought drenched me, I was like an old toy left out in the rain. My plans…

plans that I'd made in my head not even that long ago, felt like they were for nought.

Deep down I knew I had to change my mentality and my outlook, but the question that rode over me, was "What do I do now?"

I just sat, lost. Perched with my head bowed down so far, my chin touched my chest and ran adrift into a bumbling mess of what-ifs and self-doubt.

That's when it happened.

"I know, Ned. We all feel it. The pain of loss. When you get to our age, you realise that feeling never ends. It will fade, but before it can leave, something else will come along and bring it back. How you deal with it, determines how it affects you overall."

- Nanny Sawyer

ENTRY 9
IT CRACKED THE SKY

So, I was sat there, with my head sunk so low it almost met my legs as they shook, atop this familiar yet disgusting and dilapidated building of my past, when my eyes were pulled sharp to my right. It was like someone had strapped them to a jet as it took off. They'd never moved so quick.

The obnoxious sound rang through my ears as it battered them, so ferocious it reminded me of the first time I heard church bells up close.

My hands shot to cover them in an instant as the sound longed for an escape through the cramped spaces in my head. A whip and a thunderous crack, not unlike that which you get when the sound barrier breaks, only much, much louder. To me, it sounded like space had split wide open.

I looked far with the yank of my eyes as my heart slammed hard against my chest like someone had hit the brakes of a speeding car with no warning. I was blinded by the shy sun as it peaked through the clouds that had separated, and there it was.

Titan4.

Unmistakeable by the blue hue of its paint, a distinction from the green-tinted one that I'd taken sanctuary in.

It veered downward at an angle so steep that it began to progressively cast a shadow over the town I was in, like a full eclipse. Everything around me sank into darkness.

You never really see how big those things are until they're so close to you. When we queued to board them, we were all so distracted by the chaos we never took much of it all in. I noted the size of the bolts and the panels but that was as much as I remembered. And when I disembarked and put my feet back on solid ground, I quickly ran away and never looked back at it.

This... this was the whole ship, or barge, in its entirety, scarily close to me, and more so with every doomed second that passed. The entire time all I could think of was how the ship that floated above me, was way off its target zone. If it was headed for where it took off from, like mine was, anyway.

It took fifty long seconds as it disappeared past the town to the left of me and left a trail of smoke behind it. Eventually, the ground beneath me and the building I was sitting on, shook. Everything did. I'm almost certain the air quivered with me as it slapped me relentlessly in the face.

The planet trembled as Titan4 made contact with the ground in the near distance. You didn't have to be a genius to figure out that the force of the rumble and the shake of the ground weren't supposed to happen. Titan4 hadn't landed, it had crashed.

Loose dust and rubble in the mill I'd scaled, shifted, and fell as it was all given a helping hand to freedom by the quake. Then the cloud, or rather, the storm of dust and debris pushed at me with both hands as it swam into the town and knocked me from the shallow ledge that I was happy on. Whatever windows remained in the buildings around me became victim to the force of an unexpected sharp wind and fell from their frames in a million pieces as if at the push of a button.

It lasted much longer than anyone would have liked. If I was dreaming, it was a sadistic one, but the pain that shot through my bones as I lifted myself from the position I was thrown into, proved that theory mute. I was very much awake.

When the dust and the sound settled, and the hyperactive vibration of the ground had calmed, I picked myself up and ran as fast as I could.

Down the tiring steps of the mill as I jumped over the piles of ceiling slumped around, out of the building, and followed the unmissable trail of smoke down Bakersfield Close. The steps I took were fast, but nowhere near as fast as the frantic beat my heart ramped out.

I ran through every shortcut I knew about, even one particular alley that everyone called 'danger alley.'

I probably don't have to explain why it was called that… but once upon a time, it saw its fair share of criminal activity. Usually, if I ever had to, I'd walk danger alley with my head down, glued to the ground and my hands in my pockets. Instead, I had my head was pointed to the sky as I bolted through it as fast as I could, eyes fixed on the smoke as I followed it.

Another picture of proof that things weren't the same anymore.

I squeezed through gaps that had formed in fallen fences and hopped my body over the shorter ones I could handle. My aim was Titan4, and I believed I was closer than I was at the time. I kept running for as long as I could. I wasn't exactly unfit, but the distance I covered seemed like it lasted forever. I could only wonder if my brother ever felt the same feeling when he ran his marathons. That being said, he rarely complained about anything.

My pace slowed eventually, I guess I just wasn't used to how the air here differed from the manufactured air on Titan1, or maybe Earth's air was just... not the same now. But with every step forward, regardless of the speed at which they pushed me forward, I got closer and closer.

It's hard to scale things in the mind, but one thing I knew for certain was at that moment, in my panic and my rush, the town I'd lived in my whole life felt bigger than it ever had before. It had become a stranger to me, like everything within it.

That, or maybe it was some twisted manipulation of my brain as the world around me knew as well as I did, that my best friend in the entire universe, Emily, was on that ship.

"I don't really like the whole 'flying thing.' I'm more a fan of the boats and the engineering. Something about being up in the sky, piloting the wings of doom just feels unsafe to me. I'd rather be in the water, where I can swim to safety, rather than helpless in the sky."

- Emily Richards

ENTRY 10
TITAN4

Flooded from another tidal wave of emotion. Tired from a perilous chase. Confused and disoriented by another harrowing sight, I stared at the crater Titan4 had made as it rested in pain not even 500 yards outside the town. A journey cut short, as its landing zone wasn't for a further eleven miles from where it had crashed.

The dent it had made in the planet… if I was to climb down it would have been akin to traversing a canyon. The size and mass of the ship had crippled everything it had made contact with.

Smoke bellowed from exhausts the size of small cars and leaked from gaps that had been forced between mangled panels as they sparked away carelessly in their slumber. Components that either matched or exceeded my own size were scattered untidily across the field of debris.

Ironic, how I'd taken sanctuary on a ship just like it, and yet there I was, standing, watching as it had undoubtedly claimed the lives of many more people. My jaw was locked shut by fear and my eyes wouldn't close no matter how hard I tried. Instead, they observed, and fed my brain every ounce of information they could until I geared up.

Flames filled the barge. Every gap or crevice I could see was met with an orange flicker. It had levelled countless buildings in its descent; the remains of which had scarred the panels with brick score marks. It was like a monumental, blue-tinted, town-sized wrecking ball.

The side I stood and stared at for what must have been just a hundred feet away was mangled beyond recognition. Caved in from an impact so violent it was like it had been repeatedly punched by the very universe it called home. Icicles and frost sat in crowds around where panels should have been, and gaping holes now were. They began to melt under the heat of the fires within.

Titan4 had suffered an impact from something before it entered the atmosphere, that much was clear by the hole I stood and examined from afar. A hole that sat near the top part of the ship that had been untouched by the crash and collisions. Something so massive it ripped through it like a knife through butter. I don't know what it could have been, but my first and last thoughts were an asteroid. Just a dumb oversized rock slinging its way across the universe with no intentions of pumping the brakes to let humanity pass through. I couldn't say what else could have caused such a mess on such a massive spacecraft, but clearly, whatever it was wounded Titan4. Critically.

The crackles and snaps of electricity made me jump every single time they happened. They sounded like fireworks, but then the thought circled back around: it was highly unlikely that of all the 15,000 people aboard that mountain of scrap metal we once called a vessel was alive.

Friends, innocent families, hopeful for their return… Emily.

My chest collapsed upon itself as I muttered those words in silence. It couldn't be. After my hours and hours of moping and remembrance, with the knowledge that soon, Emily could share those trips with me… was it all over, just like that?

Panic rode over me like nothing I'd ever felt before. My eyes swelled up with tears that wouldn't stop, my heart thumped away fast enough to break through my chest and my legs felt like they did when I woke up six weeks prior; they could barely hold my weight. All of that time in the skies above, safe from the destruction and ruin that took our homes and our families, only to be taken away as hope is given back on your return. I couldn't process the pain.

I knew it, but I refused to believe it. It was either stubbornness or shock, but I pushed my back foot hard against the grass I was standing on and pushed myself forward. I ran as fast as my legs would take me. It was only a hundred yards, give or take, and my only real obstacle was the crater the ship had made. But all of a sudden, before I could plan my next steps, I was forced back by something so strong that it lifted my feet inches off the ground and flung me sideways over the ground I'd covered.

Titan4 had exploded.

What threw me back was the start of a volatile chain reaction that lit up the skies around me. The leftmost engine at the rear ignited, then the right, until it shot through the ship like a lightning bolt and took everything with it until all that was left as I stood back to my feet and helplessly watched, was the burning carcass of a Titan that once promised safety.

And that was it. The moment all my sinking feelings and all my fears came true. Nobody would have survived that. 15,000 people were gone before they could even think about stepping a foot back on their home turf.

The tears that tackled their way out of my eyes fell down my cheeks in a stream of sorrow and dread. Like a crack in a dam, it was challenging to even stop the leak that started, so instead, I just let it go. I had no more strength within me. I let my legs lose control as they buckled my knees… knees which left two dents in the soft grass beneath me as they plummeted down with the full weight of my body, and I let the rampaging waterfall of pain within me take control because it was stronger than me.

I'd not cried that hard since maybe four weeks after my parents died – not felt that raw pain before, and when we lost Richie, I was younger, so it never processed so emotionally, even though it hurt me. I knew I missed him, and I knew everything felt… off without him, but the tears wouldn't catch on. When I lost my parents, I felt the loss of everything they ever did for me, and when I lost my grandparents to this new-age madness we were all subjected to, it hurt… but I was given plenty of warning, so it hurt just a little bit less. Titan4, however… I'd just watched as the ship that carried not only my best friend – the best person on this planet, Emily, and also a tenth of the remaining human population, crashed.

I may as well have stayed here when it all kicked off. That was the thought that rotated through my head.

I could have watched tsunamis rip entire cities apart, earthquakes take countless lives and superstorms uproot and mangle towns and cities as they left nothing but a massacre in their wake.

They would have all claimed just as many lives in just as little time.

I must have passed out, because the next thing I remember is being woken up from a slump right there on the grass, less than a hundred feet away from hell. First, I saw the tatty denim jeans, then the grey jumper. I didn't recognise his face as he held his hand out to aid me up.

"Are you alright, son?" he asked me.

I couldn't physically talk back to him, even though I tried to.

I was either concussed from the blast or the pain that consumed me was so brutal it robbed me of even my most basic functions, so I just grunted as I grabbed the hand that reached to me and pulled myself up with its aid.

I thought my legs felt weird minutes ago as they wobbled beneath me, but that was nothing. I was standing, but I couldn't feel them, I felt like I was floating, almost. Numb to the core - I felt dead, whilst clearly alive, practically a zombie. I mean, I may as well have been one at that point. Everything else I'd encountered had become one.

The man who helped me wasn't the only one there. The crash of Titan4 was so loud and invasive that it took the attention of everyone who had returned with me. After hours of escaping them all, I found myself back there.

Philip was there. The man who always made sure I was okay. The grey in his hair was illuminated by the fires he was staring into. He was separated from the remaining crowd that stood by and cried. Parents screaming, friends and family were on their knees just as I was.

But Philip… Philip just sunk his knees into the grass and bellowed out into the skies in a scream so loud and pained it scared the life out of me. I ran over to him… it was a little bit difficult, given how dodgy my legs were at the time.

I skipped over the uneven ground like an injured horse, but I managed it. Why run to him? I'm sure if you're reading this you can remember, when I met Philip on Titan1, he told me about his son, a young son that had been separated from him and placed on Titan4. Six-year-old Tobias.

I sat down beside him, though, it was more of a drop down, and I wrapped my arms around him. Even through all of the pain that I carried myself at that moment, I couldn't begin to imagine his. I hugged him for what seemed like an eternity, he needed it, just one arm around his shoulders to pull him in, and with the deepest, shakiest breath I ever drew, I asked him a question I never got the chance to on Titan1.

"Was he with his mum?"

The stocky man wept into my shoulder. I felt his chest rip itself apart as he muttered the few words he had left through his tears.

"No, she left us when he was three."

A mother who left him… six years of age… stashed onto a ship and separated from his father, his only parent. Promised safety and a return, but it was all more of the string of lies they'd told.

Because of the dumbfounded and ridiculous way in which our governments structured the boarding of the Titans, Philip's son was ripped away from him in the moments when he was all he had left. Six, tiny years old and instead of Philip welcoming him home with a hug full of life and love, a future ahead of them… he was now stuck, fixed down in that field, mourning him.

I let his head sink further into my shoulder as his world fell apart.

A ship, full of children and families, friends, and associates. Emily. A massive metal container containing thousands of lives. A promise, broken by a freak accident on entry.

This, I remember thinking. This is the world we live in now.

Fuck this world.

"We, as a united body, will do everything in our power to protect those that live among us. It may not be a smooth ride, but it will be a ride, nonetheless. You will be protected, and you will be one with the rest of us. No one person shall be thrown aside and cast upon the line that baits destruction.

We are a world. We are humanity. As such, we will work together to overcome that which awaits. From this moment forward, we are a family."

- Sylvia Therman, Secretary of the Titan Initiative, Professional Liar.

ENTRY 11
EMILY

Yeah, I talk about her a lot. As you would too if you knew her.

Anyway, I'd sat on the grass with Philip, easily for an hour before Suzie found him and took over the role of comforter. From her, such an approach was more suited than that from me; someone who had no idea what to say next. I only hope he'd be okay.

A group of suits from the top deck of Titan1 decided they were the leaders of us all now and led us all to a multi-storey block of flats downtown, just a mile from the catastrophe that crippled us all. Apparently, it was where they'd begun to set up camp when Titan4 crashed.

It was battered, riddled with moss and weather, but it worked. I couldn't help but wonder if the place they'd led us to, much like the Titans, also was masked with lies and anarchy.

It took me quite a long time, longer than I'll ever admit on paper, but as I scanned around the complex, began to recognise it. I'd been there before, years ago.

It was where Emily's sister, Regan used to live. I don't even know if Regan made it to a Titan, she and Emily fell out a year ago and refused to speak to each other. All I know of that entire mess is that Regan's partner, Ted, wasn't exactly the bundle of 'loyalty' that he claimed to be, and Regan wouldn't hear Emily's side of it, so they parted ways.

I ended up bunkering down in 'Flat 2b" on the second floor of five.

There was a bettered sofa in an otherwise bare living room that stank of age, and even though it looked damp and rotten, I sat on it anyway. I needed to rest my legs, my body… I needed to rest everything. I slouched as I used to at home on my bed when I'd subject myself to laziness and shut reality out.

All I could think about was Emily. So, to immortalise her, I want you to know the kind of person she was, why I talk about her with such fondness, and why I genuinely loved her as much as I did. I'll keep it as short as I can, because I know full well, that I can talk about this woman forever.

Me and her were born on the same ward, in the same hospital in Henchester, just four weeks apart. Nancy, her mum, went to school with mine. Just like me and Emily, those two were good friends.

We never realised how tight we would become when we started nursery together – the innocence of youth just kept us close in a class of twelve hyperactive children.

In primary school - that's when we grew a lot closer. We shared a lot of the same classes: English, Art, P.E, most of them. We were rarely apart.

I got bullied a lot back then because I had a lot of anxiety issues, so I'd be distant, quiet… a perfect target for bullies. But Emily was a different breed than I was. She was loud, defensive, and stood her ground as I only wished I could.

She'd taken a beatdown to three of the four guys who bullied me within the first three weeks of starting year 3.

She would always ask if I was okay and sit with me at dinner where we'd talk about literally anything and everything, and she'd even walk home with me. Even though she lived on the other side of our small town, she'd walk with me to my gate, say hello to my mum and dad, and then walk back home. I knew as early as then that we'd be friends forever. Sometimes you can just feel it.

When we were thirteen years old, Emily lost her nan. It was a heart attack in the early month of May. It led her to a triple-bypass operation, but she never fully recovered from it.

In the same week, I fractured my collarbone falling off my bike at the local park. My mum rang Nancy, and to distract her from the pain of losing her mother, she brought up the accident I'd had. Within thirty minutes of my mum mentioning it, Emily was at our doorstep. She'd called in to check on me after Nancy passed on the news of my clumsiness.

She'd just lost her nan, but there she was, checking on me and my brittle collar bone. Me… when I lose people, I shut the world out, as I've said quite often, but not her. Emily knew the world kept turning no matter what happened, and she accepted, or at least, dealt with things on a level I could only dream of. Like right now, for instance, as I write this, the strength she had in her, is a strength I could really do with.

Oh, she was about as positive as you could get, too. She had her off days, just like everyone else, Except, on her off days, it was more than a clever idea to not look her directly in the eyes. She wasn't a 'bark's worse than the bite,' person. You had to watch out for both. If you liked your jaw to remain fixed in its position, you'd leave her alone.

Ask Toby. Ask him about the day he mocked her for dying her hair red like most of the other girls did. Ask him how long his nose bled for after she punched him, twice. I'd never heard someone apologise so often in so few days.

Everything Emily loved… the world knew about. She was ever so proud of her uncle Ronnie; he was in the navy… the uncle she wanted to follow in her own pursuit. He was a jet pilot, but Emily didn't want to be one of those, she was more interested in the boats, but she sang his praises every chance she got, because even though she didn't want to follow him directly, she understood his bravery and his role.

And her mother. Nancy was a carer for the elderly, she'd rotate laps around the town visiting her patients from seven in the morning until six in the evening. It was a role a lot of people turned their eyes at, yet a role that none of them would do themselves, despite being paid to.

The fact is it didn't matter what you did. If you were a good person and she saw value in you, Emily would love you with zero discrimination. To be a part of that circle of trust and love was an honour that nothing else could match.

On my seventeenth birthday, she even bought me a new phone. My old one was practically as old as the house I was raised in, and I never considered asking my parents for a new one because I simply chose new games consoles or money above it all.

Emily… well, she'd saved money from her part-time cleaning job and outright bought me one. No strings, no motives. Keep in mind, I'd not gotten my retail job yet, that was a few months down the line, again, with her help as she kicked my lazy arse into gear.

As you can already imagine, even in the short notes I've made of her, she was the purest, strongest, and most selfless person I knew. Anyone else who knew her shared the exact same opinion as me. She, alongside my parents, was the reason I grew up. She was another bright beacon that would guide me, and she was my forever friend. In our old age, in our seventies, I imagined we'd still be joined at the hip, and now even that was gone.

I can still smell her hair. The same coconut shampoo she used to wash it with. It sounds creepy as I read it in my head, but it's one of those things you don't know until it's gone. Just another staple of her presence that fit this beautiful jigsaw together. Her perfume, too. A gift from Ronnie, her uncle. I can't explain the smell as well as I wish I could. Sweet, I think jasmine... and sandalwood?

You'd always see her before you... *saw* her, you know? Twi clustered gems hung from the studs pinned into her ears that would slingshot sunlight right back at you like a laser.

The chipped canine tooth on her upper right set, from where she tried to ego-challenge me with the lid of a shandy bottle when we were 16. The quirk of the chip grew on her.

Her laugh. The gentle snort she'd make after her lungs emptied with a full-bellied laugh. How she'd wind it down with an exertion that sounded like the bass note of a flute. The twitch of her eye and the flare of her right nostril when she'd get mad. As I said, I could go on forever, she really was that special to me. Through nothing more than her existence.

The day before we boarded the Titans, she sent me a message. I'm sure I brought that up earlier, but at the time I chose to keep it to myself.

Sometimes you just need something to hold on to. I guess deep down I was saving it for when something, anything inevitably went wrong. But she messaged me. My phone may be dead and as useless as most electronics now, but I remember that message as if it were tattooed at the forefront of my brain. The words lie on the cusp of my memories like a glorious entrance banner.

>HEY SHITHEAD,
>
>GONNA MISS YOU, YOU KNOW
>
>IT'S GONNA FEEL LIKE FOREVER
>
>BUT I'LL SEE YOU SOON (I PROMISE)
>
>MIFFED I'M ON 4, BUT WHATEVER, RIGHT?
>
>LOVE YA,
>
>SEE YOU WHEN WE GET BACK HOME
>
>XOX

And that… that's what death really is, how it feels. It's that sensation when someone you love says 'see you when we get back home,' and you hang onto the words in anticipation of their fruition. Then that hope that it creates within you gets snatched away in an instant, and you don't know what to do with what's left. Because they won't see you soon, and they won't be coming back home.

When my brother left for his trip, he said, "See you when I get back," then joked, "If I ever do." He never did.

When my parents left for their holiday, Dad said, "Look after the house, we'll be back before you know it."

"Don't come back," I joked. But they never did come back.

When I left for Titan1, my head told me I would see my grandparents again. My grandad said to me, "It won't be forever." In reality, it was.

My nan said, "We'll be right here when you get back." Only their spirits were, not them.

Emily's last message to me carried the same fate as the others did. She told me that she'd see me soon, she told me she'd be back home. I replied with only a few words that day:

>I'LL MISS YOU TOO
>
>SEE YOU WHEN IT'S ALL OVER, EMZ
>
>I'M SO SCARED

I was scared. She was probably the only person I would admit fear to. But this planet could burn beneath my feet, it could toss and turn in its wildest nightmare, and it could throw the tantrum of a millennium. It still wouldn't scare me as much as knowing I would live out whatever remained of my life, on a gigantic space rock where my number one person wouldn't be there with me. The fear of boarding day was minuscule compared to what I feel as I write this.

The circle of life, only they never tell you it's not a simple circle. Instead, it's a ring of fire that closes in around you. It burns everything you've witnessed in life and everything you hold close until it finally gets to you: its final target.

At least, that's how I saw it all, anyway.

I better end this one here, I can feel myself veer off into a darkness I don't want you to witness. I need a moment to gather my senses. Everything's so noisy right now as it is, with all the people moving about and making homes out of these abused flats.

I'm exhausted, my brain is shattered into a billion pieces, and they're handing out food they'd carted off of Titan1.

I'll rest, check on Philip, Suzie, and Toby, then I'll be back. I hope.

"He was the brightest light on Earth, and now he's the brightest star in the sky. Sprinkled with thousands of companions that will lead him to a glorious afterlife, I wish nothing for them all, and him, but to find love in the heavens that his home couldn't give."

- Philip Macintosh, Remembering Tobias

"I don't know what life is without you. Because you were my life. I can't think of or remember a day when you weren't at my side, making me feel human in a world where I felt alien. Love has a whole new meaning when you hold infinite quantities of it for someone so special."

- Ned Sawyer, Remembering Emily

ENTRY 12
THRIVE? OR SURVIVE?

I've left it a few days since I last wrote something. The pain of remembering Emily hit me pretty hard, I spent most of the time that followed the remembrance ceremony, sleeping. Dreams of her face and what it felt like to be her friend. Nightmares of the days that will come to pass, knowing she should be here but isn't. I'm not the only one. So many people in this building with me have been going through the same. If I remember, I'll put some notes of the speeches that were made between the last entry and this. Philip's was beautiful. It tells you a lot about a man when he loses his only son, but in remembering him, remembers everyone else that was lost with him.

Parents attended without their children and vice-versa. Friends who vowed to see each other again were shattered as obituaries were written or voiced. It's all been one big mess as we all struggled to process what had happened to Titan4.

The 'officials' went out there. A few times. They confirmed what we all already knew: nobody had survived. It was obvious enough, it burned for 18 hours straight until the rainstorm came and eventually put it all out. Then it took another six hours for the metal structure to be cooled enough to approach.

They set up their little operation and cordoned off the area with a few makeshift guards. Random people were chosen to fulfil the duty with the promise of bonus rations like they were all dogs working for a handful of treats.

They didn't want anybody seeing what lay inside the ship. Not that anybody wanted to see anything other than their loved ones one last time. All I can say is I lost count of the number of corpses they dragged out of there and lay next to it. A mound, like something of a horror movie where all the victims lay on display. Why they couldn't leave them in there I will never know. They used whatever tarps and sheets lay about to cover it and weighed them down with debris from the crash. Philip donated his red blanket to the cause. He only asked one thing in return, that they wrap his son in it when they found him. What surprised me most, is they did just that and they honoured Philip.

They identified Tobias by the watch he wore. A thirty-year-old leather-strapped timepiece. A watch Philip said he'd given him.

"Every time that big hand ticks is a second closer to seeing me again," he told Tobias. It was true, and also beautiful, whilst another case of what I already discussed; cursed words in the last moments of a loved one.

I both can and can't imagine what's been going through Philip's head, but every time I looked across the rooms, and every time I saw that mound of bodies in my wanders outside the block of flats, I can't help but admit how wrong I've really been.

Things were never going to go back to the way they were. At least, not the future that awaited me. Hell-bent on going back home, rebuilding, and pretending like none of this ever happened? That was never realistic. A bad call and a bad plan. The people around me needed me, as much as I needed them, only I was too ignorant to see that in my time on Titan1. I know I made a promise to my parents at St. Peter's, but maybe I can honour it in a different way.

'Home,' isn't necessarily the house I grew up in, or the town I was raised in, but rather the planet it was all built on. To rebuild home, would be to rebuild humanity. It was right there in front of me the entire time, my mum said it to e once, in almost identical words. Maybe it's something else I'll use as a quote to end an entry. Maybe by the time you get this far, I've already used it.

I wouldn't know where to start. Through the masses of tears, the weight of torment and dread, and the ever-looming presence of Titan4's carcass in the near distance reminding us of how easily our pitiful numbers can be slashed, it was all a lot to take in. It was like being birthed late into a new world order where even the smartest people were dumbfounded by it all.

I knelt beside the sheets on the floor where we slept last night, and I prayed.

I hoped Emily would hear the prayers. My parents and grandparents, too. I promised I would do better in my second chance on this ball of rock.

I hoped my grandparents would her when I said I would do everything in my power to prove their deaths weren't for nothing. That the world could be born again, and this time humanity would get it right.

I hoped my parents would hear how serious I was when I said once more that I would rebuild, only this time, not necessarily the house. The people. That I would make them all proud. And I told Emily how all of this is for them, the future, and her alike.

Heavy promises from someone who barely survived a retail assistant job, I know. But promises and persistence are all I have left right now. The best I can do is live out the rest of my days seeing them true, to the best of my ability. I was never alone in it, the people around me were people I once was desperate to escape, but life works in mysterious ways, and they were around me once more.

That means something.

I know whoever… if anyone, reads this, it can't have been easy to get this far. To follow in my footsteps as I stepped off Titan1 with a strong belief that everything would be daisies and rainbows. But this is what life is now. Misery and loss. Living from the bare minimum.

You're probably part of a younger generation born into it, holding your eyes on it all in a more innocent light because it's all you know.

Maybe you're reading this far into the future, and everything is teeming with life and productivity once again. Or maybe nobody is reading this.

Whichever it is, I hope I succeeded even a little bit, in making it a smoother ride for you, than it ever was for my family, my friends, Philip, or me. Any of us.

To call on the obvious, my return wasn't the glee I convinced myself it would be. The trips down memory lane (or avenue…) were great, but not in the way they should have been. But regardless, I made it home. Rather than write more jargon on this paper and push myself further into a state of denial, I figure it's time I thought about doing something. Something real, and impactful.

The other Titans will be touching down soon. Titan 3 already landed in Wisconsin, and Titan 7 safely returned to Sydney, which leaves 6 more to join us and start over.

They'll need us, as we will them. If there's one thing I do know now, it's that they don't understand what awaits them, none of us really did.

The first thing any Titan touching down on this side of the planet will see is the massacre of Titan4. It can hardly be missed; it would be like saying you can't see Everest.

It won't sit well. It'll gnaw away at them, the same way it does with everyone inside the flats.

Reader,

Your future will be bright. Because mine was stolen. Everything I thought would be, ceased to exist the second I signed that boarding pass. Now, I choose to fight day by day to make sure not a single one of them is wasted.

We should take care of our home. As disappointing and hell-driven as it can be. The fact remains.

Next time, we may not return at all.

"We pass through this world but once. Few tragedies can be more extensive than the stunting of life, few injustices deeper than the denial of an opportunity to strive or even to hope, by a limit imposed from without, but falsely identified as lying within."

- Stephen Jay Gould

ENTRY 13
EIGHTEEN MONTHS

I almost forgot this journal existed. Much like the rest of the items in my bag, it got lost at the bottom. Having found it, I wanted to make an addition, and see how things compare now.

To start, it's been a year and a half since my last entry.

A lot has changed.

Every Titan has safely landed in the time that has passed. Most people chose to build around the Titans and use them as landmarks almost. Humanity's second arrival. A monument that would set a stamp in history and define our era.

I still reflect on my juvenile lack of conception back when I first landed on my return here. I almost feel sorry for myself and where my head was at.

For over a year now I've been part of a team. One team of many brave souls. Me, Philip, Toby, Suzie, and a few other people who'd joined along the way. We've been restoring the buildings around us. Ripping up carpets and removing old furniture, building new from scraps of whatever decent wood remained, and making homes. So far, we've covered an entire section of the town we now call 'Haven.' The name's pretty fitting, actually.

Oh! Some news also…

Philip and Suzie got really close in the first few months working together, they became an 'item.'

To cut a long but beautiful story short, Suzie is now five months pregnant as I write this. They have their ideas on the name of the child. But, seeing as they have no way of determining the sex of it, they planned accordingly:

If it's a girl, they want to call her Emily.

Emily Rosanne Baker.

In honour of my fallen friend, Suzie's mother and obviously, Philip's surname, in respective order.

If it's a boy, they'll call him Arnie Tobias Baker.

Named after Suzie's brother and Philip's never-forgotten son.

Even in a world of chaos, sparks of light like that can happen, and baby Emily or Arnie have no idea just how strong the love for them will be on their arrival. After all, in mourning, love will shine the brightest on things anew. Well, that's what Suzie told me anyway, she's lovely. She reminds me a lot of my Auntie Marnie with her sweet demeanour. She and Philip make an incredible team.

I wish I had some good news about Sylvia, but she disappeared into one of the towers with her followers and left us all in the dust. I imagine she's plotting away, people like her always do. Sometimes, as hard as it is to chew, people like her just get away with what they do. I fully believe one day she'll get exactly what she deserves, they all will. But that's no longer my concern, my new family is. Priorities are what make or break you now.

I am now hopeful for what the future can bring. More than I once was, and it's because of a little thing called progress.

In teamwork comes advancement, and in advancement comes a promising future. For example, the flats which we once bunkered down in, and used the floors as beds… they now have real beds built within them, and mattresses made from knitted together sheets. It's hardly perfect, but it's a major difference from sleeping on rotted floors.

Food is looking better, too. For a long time, we were convinced we'd run out, but a group of people strolled around the gardens and fields and found a healthy number of seeds. Now, we have patches where we grow fresh food. Lots of them. The officials obviously wanted to start charging for the food to get a cycle of currency floating through the system again, but we were far from willing to listen to them any longer. I don't know where they all went, and I don't care.

All I care about is the people around me. To use Sylvia's own words against her, we are a family. Initiative cronies are not included.

I understand that with how few people remain, my involvement in that future grows bigger the longer we thrive. Though, I wonder, are we really thriving? Or right now, is it a case of survival, even after the past 18 months? As you can tell, a lot of what surrounds us is still open to debate and question. Uncertainty is a thing that unites us all, brings us all closer and helps us understand we're all in it together.

I will see it through regardless, as I have already, and I have no intention of hitting the brakes. This planet is my home, these people are my family, and you, you as you read this… are a part of that ever-growing family. I'm doing this for you, and I only hope we did you proud.

FINAL WORDS

Dear reader,
The world you were born into is a different one from what I was. I hope you understand this.

I saw the collapse, I saw the return, and I participated in the rebirth.

Please don't do what we did and take it all for granted, that's not what it's for. Instead, whatever your situation and whatever the community around you looks like, welcome it like it's your best friend. You will never understand the value of these people until it's far too late, trust me on that one. Love it and the people around you. Life's lesson is a harsh one, yet a simple one. Days are numbered, and only the heavens above know what those numbers are, so treat every day as though it's your last and use your life to pave the greatness for what follows it.

I wrote this journal, initially to record my footsteps as I looked back on my home, my family, and my childhood. It quickly turned into a way to provide immortality for the memories and ended as a plea to the future. But I'm forever thankful I had this notepad and these pens in the bag I took with me to Titan1, because now, you, the new generation, can have a slice of what I once did. Normality.

You may have noticed each entry is closed with a quote. Some famous, some personal. I added those after the fact, as I wrote this section. I want you to read them, so you can see as I do, how foolish I was with each step of my journey.

Also, so you can see that your parents, grandparents and loved ones alike, all share one thing in common: their capacity for knowledge. You'll notice the people I held close gave me these lessons once upon a time, but I was too blind to see it. Too narrow-minded to understand what they meant. I urge you to not do the same.

Whatever happens between now and you reading this, I hold faith that you'll continue it. Not as we did, but better. Advance.

This is Ned Sawyer, and these were my memoirs of home.

Of Earth.

"You know, Noddy, I know you just want to sit and play games all day. I know what you're like. You're not a people person. Do you know what my uncle Ronnie once told me?

He said that laziness is the catalyst for wonder. When all you do is sit back and kick your feet up, those four, five hours… are missed opportunities. You grow into it, get used to it, and before you know it, you're seventeen years old with no job and no money. Get off your arse, Noddy. The world ain't waiting for you."

- Emily Richards, circa 2023

I'll see you in another life, Emily.

END
OF
JOURNAL

THANK YOU FOR READING

Printed in Great Britain
by Amazon